Mrs. Archibald Little

The fairy Foxes

A chinese legend

Mrs. Archibald Little

The fairy Foxes
A chinese legend

ISBN/EAN: 9783743355316

Manufactured in Europe, USA, Canada, Australia, Japa

Cover: Foto ©Andreas Hilbeck / pixelio.de

Manufactured and distributed by brebook publishing software
(www.brebook.com)

Mrs. Archibald Little

The fairy Foxes

Printed by T. HASEGAWA, 10 Hiyoshicho, Tokio, Japan.

The Fairy Hares.

MORE than a thousand years ago, when the Tangs were rulling over, China, there lived a young man, whose name was Chin Wang, and who came from the Capital. He had read no learned books, and was not fond of study, but was very fond of wine and good cheer, and he managed a sword better than most men; but what he liked best of all was galloping about armed with a Crossbow.

Chin Wang lost his father when he was still young, and as he had only his mother left, he married. His younger brother Say Wang was extraordinarily strong, and never found his match in military exercises; so he took service among the Emperor's guards, and did not think of marrying. These two young men had a brilliant fortune; a great number of servants obeyed their orders, and they found themselves in an assured position promising every happiness.

But all on a sudden a revolt broke out. The defile between the mountains and the Yellow River being unprovided with a garrison, the Emperor found it necessary to retire to the West, and Say Wang was one of the escort who accompanied the fugitive Emperor. As for Chin Wang, thinking that he could not live on in the same way in the Capital, when it had fallen into the power of the rebels, he abandoned his property, and, gathering together all the things that it was possible to take away, carried off his mother, his wife and his servants, and, going South, established himself in a small village near Hang-Chow, where he occupied himself looking after the land he had bought round his house.

At last Chin Wang heard that the Capital had been retaken by the Emperor's troops, and that the roads were safe; and the idea came into his head to go back there to learn what had become of his friends and relations, and put his former property in order. Having made up his mind to set out, he told his mother and his wife, arranged his baggage, and having taken leave like a respectful son, started, taking with him only one servant, called Fo. · At first he travelled by boat, but at last he arrived at a most important point, where two rivers meet, and which is like the key to the roads from the north and the south; the masts of boats coming and going are crowded there like ears of corn in a field, all the banks are covered with houses close to one another, and there is a never-ceasing gathering of buyers and sellers, so that the whole place is full of gaiety and movement.

Now it was precisely there that Chin had to leave his boat to continue his journey by land. He bought mules to carry his baggage, and adopted the costume of an army officer. As he went along he gazed with pleasure on the rivers and mountains, and at night slept soundly. Thus he travelled on till he came to a village not far from the Capital. All the families, which had inhabited it, had fled away or hidden; there was not one inhabited house along the roadside, and barely a traveller, so that all that Chin saw was:-

"The high tops of the hills, which the forests wrapt in shadow; the high, poetic peaks of the mountains, whose tops cleft the azure sky. In the midst of precipitous rocks and of mountains reaching far into the distance, the river Han winding in a limpid stream; the sheet of water in a slanting course precipitating its silvery waves ten thousand feet; creepers hanging over the abyss, and the breeze making them float like an embroidered scarf of many colours. Over the immense extent of mountains, lost among the clouds, narrow footpaths made rather for birds than men, and which the rare traveller can only follow stooping till he is almost bent double; the misty forests mingling with the clouds; the ravaged villages all solitary, man having disappeared from the deserted country, dressed in a thousand colours by the mountain flowers wide open in their gladness, birds alone disturbing the solitude unknown with their cries.

Chin Wang, entranced by the beauty of the smiling scene, rode forward, letting the reins hang upon his horse's neck, when towards evening, just when the sky was growing dark he heard in the depths of the forest something that sounded like human voices. He drew nearer and o looked. It was not men, it was two wild

Told in English by Mrs. Archibald Little.

Foxes, who, leaning against the trunk of an old tree, held before them a written book. Each with one paw pointing at the writing, they were talking just as two men would do when discussing a doubtful passage.

"Ah!" cried Chin Wang laughing, "these two animals are wonderful indeed, they must be fairies! But what can be the book, that is so interesting them? Supposing I was to give them one of my bullets?" And thereupon tightening his silken reins to stop his horse, he gently raised the end of the bridle ornamented with polished horn, arranged the string of the crossbow, plunged his hand into his pocket, and took from it a bullet, that he placed in the barrel, then aimed with the greatest care; the crossbow grew round like the moon at the full, the bullet whistled flying with the rapidity of a falling star. The two Foxes, engaged in a study that was full of interest for them, had no idea that someone was spying upon them from beyond the skirts of the forest; at the whistling of the cord of the crossbow they raised their heads to see where the noise came from; but in its rapid flight, turning neither to the right nor to the left, the ball at once went right into the middle of the left eye of the Fox who held the book.

The poor beast dropped the Manuscript with piercing cries, and ran away with its wound; the other Fox was already stooping to pick up the book left by its companion, when a second bullet from Chin struck it on the right temple; it then also ran away with loud cries, as if flying from death. The traveller pushed forward his horse, and ordered his servant to pick up the book; but when he examined it, he found that its pages were covered with letters made like tadpoles, and all quite impossible for him to read.

Chin thought to himself "I don't know at all what is written in this book, but I will carry it off, and by-and-bye at my leisure consult some learned man who can read ancient writings." At once he hid the manuscript in his sleeve, trotted out of the forest, and took the high road leading to the Capital.

Now at this time it is true that one of the leaders of the insurrection was dead, but his son was quite as much to be feared. Another of the leaders had just revolted again; everywhere powerful forces were gathered together; nowhere were there signs of the rebels returning to their allegiance; and as they were afraid some of the rebels might come as far as the Capital to spy out the measures of the Government, there was watch and ward kept at the gates. All those who came in or went out were subjected to a severe examination, and directly it was dusk the gates were shut. When Chin arrived at the foot of the wall, the sun was already set, and the bolts were shut; he had therefore to find a resting-place for the night.

Arrived at the door of an inn he got off his horse and entered. The Innkeeper, seeing a stranger with a crossbow and a sword, dressed like an officer, took care not to receive him coldly, but going to meet him with politeness, begged him to take a seat. The servants had orders to bring a cup of tea, and meanwhile his own servant, Fo, brought the baggage into the house.

"Have you a safe and convenient room," asked Chin Wang of the Innkeeper, "that you can give me?"

"I have plenty," replied the Innkeeper, "your Lordship has but to choose which suits you." And thereupon, lighting a lamp, the Innkeeper conducted his guest through all his apartments. What suited Chin Wang best was a little room, clean and well kept, in which his things were placed, whilst the mules were taken to the stable to be looked after.

Hardly was the traveller installed before the little servant of the inn came to ask if his Lordship would take a cup of wine. "If you have good wine," answered Chin, "bring me two measures, with a plate of hashed beef. And see that everyone here obeys my orders carefully." The servant went away promising that his Lordship should be obeyed in everything. Chin, after having taken care to shut the door behind him, was going out of the room when the servant reappeared, wanting to know if his Lordship would take his repast in the public room or in his own room. "I will eat here," replied the traveller, and at once what he had ordered was put before him.

Chin Wang sat down, and his servant Fo, standing behind him, poured out the wine.

He had only drunk two or three glasses, when the Innkeeper came to know if his Lordship came from the frontier. "No," replied Chin, "I come from the South." "Nevertheless," objected the Innkeeper, "your Lordship's accent is not that of the South." "Well," said Chin, "I will speak frankly: I am originally from the Capital. But since the rebellion has compelled the Emperor to be a fugitive, I have left my home to escape trouble in the South. They say now the rebels are subdued, and the Emperor coming back, so I am going to try to repair the damage my property must have suffered, and then I am going to fetch my family. As I feared meeting with some hostility on the way, I adopted the uniform of an army officer." "Well," replied the Innkeeper," your Lordship and I are in the same case: it is not more than a year since I came to seek a refuge in this village." And as they were both compatriots, both coming from the Capital, although strangers to one another, they became like old friends, telling each other all they knew of these disastrous troubles! Well do they say:

> The hills, the streams, the winds remain
> > Just what they've always been;
> The Families of the country side
> > No longer now are seen.

Their conversation was very animated, when they heard a voice from outside saying: "Innkeeper, have you a room for the night?" " Yes!" answered the host, "but I do not know how many you are." "Only one" replied the voice; "I am quite alone."

The Innkeeper saw indeed one man alone, and without any luggage, and he answered: "Since you are without a companion I dare not receive you."

"Are you afraid perhaps that I should not pay you?" cried the new-comer very angrily. "Is that why you will not open the door to me?"

"Sir," said the Innkeeper, "that is not my reason; but the noble Captain of the Garrison has published everywhere a proclamation forbidding Innkeepers to give shelter to any unknown or suspicious traveller. Anyone accused of lodging such an one would expose himself to the severest punishment. And since this last outbreak the orders are the more peremptory. Besides, Sir, you are without baggage. I have not the advantage of knowing you, it would therefore not do at all for me to receive you."

"Why," cried the Unknown, smiling, "don't you know me? I am the Captain of the Garrison. Business called me away I am now returning. It is too late for me to get into the city, I am therefore obliged to ask you for an asylum for this night. You see therefore, why I have no baggage. But if you still have any doubts, come with me to-morrow morning as far as to the gates of the Capital, and ask the guard There is not one who does not know me.

Thanks to the great official cap, which the stranger exhibited as he bowed, the Innkeeper believed his words. "Excuse an old man for not recognising his Captain," he said, "do not be angry on account of my refusal, but come and take a seat." "Do not trouble yourself," replied the new-comer. "Only I am dying of hunger.

If you have some wine and rice I should like a little." Thereupon he entered at once, saying to the Innkeeper, "I don't eat meat, all I want is some rice and wine." Then he went and sat down at the table at which the other traveller was sitting. The servant brought what had been ordered.

Chin Wang, looking at the new arrival, noticed that he was hiding his left eye under the folds of his sleeve, shewing signs of the most extreme suffering; nevertheless it was he who broke the silence. "Mine host," said he to the Innkeeper, "I have been very unfortunate to-day. I met two rascally animals, which caused me to fall and lose my eye."

"Why! what animals did you meet?" asked the Innkeeper.

"Listen," continued the pretended Captain, "as I was coming along I saw two wild Foxes springing from side to side and calling out. I ran to catch them, when suddenly my foot caught. The two Foxes continued running, and I fell so roughly that the ball of my eye is seriously hurt."

"I was surprised to see," said the Innkeeper, "that

your Excellency hid half your face in your sleeve."

"Coming along the same road as you did," interrupted Chin Wang, "I also came across two Foxes."

"Did you manage to catch them?" asked the stranger eagerly. "They were in the forest, very attentively looking at a manuscript," replied Chin. "I sent a bullet into the left eye of the one who held the book; he dropped it and ran away. The other was going to pick up the old book, but a second bullet from my crossbow wounded his cheek, and he fled. Thus I only got the book, and the two beasts escaped me."

"What!" cried the stranger and the Innkeeper both at once, "Foxes, who know how to read! That is a strange story!"

"And in this book," asked the new-comer, "what was there written? Could I have a look at it?"

"Oh, it is a very strange book," said Chin, "there is not even one letter one can read in it." And forgetting his wine-cup, he took from his sleeve the mysterious book to shew it. But what it takes a long time to tell was quick in the doing! His hand had not yet reached his sleeve, when the grandson of the Innkeeper, a child of 5 or 6 years old, came running up, and the child's bright eyes saw at once that the stranger was a Fox. He took care not to let out what he saw too soon, but ran straight up to the animal, and pointing at the false Commandant, cried out, "Father, look at this wild Fox sitting here! and you are not hunting it away!"

Directly on hearing this Chin Wang recognised the Fox he had wounded; he seized his sword, but the animal, seeing himself in danger, avoided the sword by turning head over heels, and, appearing in its natural form, escaped from the room all breathless. Chin pursued it sword in hand past several houses, but the Fox's footsteps led him straight to the foot of a high wall. It was a dark night, and Chin could find no door, so he was obliged to come back, when the master of the inn, accompanied by his servant Fo, met him with a lighted lantern, and both begged him to spare the life of the poor animal, and not to trouble himself more about it.

"But," said Chin, "if your little grandson had not found him out I do believe the changeling would have got his book back."

"Those creatures know all sorts of tricks," interrupted the landlord, "I shall not be surprised if he invents some other magic to get back what you have taken from him."

"Anyway," said Chin, "this adventure with the Fox will be a subject for raillery with numbers of people. I must cut the hateful creature in two with my sword; then only will people leave off laughing at me."

He then returned to the inn; but the travelling merchants in the rooms to the right and left, having heard of what had passed, thought it so astonishing, they all gathered round him to hear how it had all happened; and they asked so many questions that his throat ached and his mouth felt parched.

After having supped, Chin went back to his room to take some rest; and he thought to himself that, since the Fox seemed so anxious to get back his book, it must be a treasure, so he determined to keep it hidden as carefully as possible. About mid-night he heard a tapping at his door, and a voice that said: "Quick! quick! give me back my book, and I will find a way to shew my gratitude to you. But if you do not choose to give it up, dreadful things will happen to you. Do not therefore lay up for yourself matter for regret in the future."

These words put Chin into a great rage; he threw on his clothes, seized his sword, and went out of his room quite gently, so as not to awaken his neighbours. But at the moment when he was about to open the great door of the inn he saw that the landlord had been down and locked it. "Before I have roused him, and he has got up to open all these bolts," thought Chin Wang, "this wretch of a fox will have got away, and I shall not be able to transfix him with my sword. I shall have provoked the displeasure of those who sleep near me all for nothing. It will be better to swallow my anger for the moment, and to-morrow morning I must think what to do."

So he went back to his room, and arranged himself

to sleep as before, but the Fox began his lamentations again and again, so that every man in the inn heard them. And next morning they came in a body to Chin Wang, and said: "Since you cannot read a single word in this book, what is the use in keeping it? Give it back, then, and all will yet go well! If you don't, for certain some mischief will befall you, and then you will be sorry."

If Chin Wang had known what would happen, he would have followed this advice, and given the book back to the Fairy Fox. All would then have gone well. But no! he was a proud, obstinate man, and would not listen to anyone. And in the end the magical Fox, growing embittered, took a malicious pleasure in ruining him thoroughly. They say with truth :—

> If wise men's voice you scorn to hear
> You'll surely shed a bitter tear!

After breakfast Chin Wang paid his bill; his baggage was placed upon the mules; he mounted on horseback and entered into the Capital. Everywhere where he looked round him he saw houses in ruins and scarcely an inhabitant; the open places and the markets were sad and deserted. What a difference from the brilliant appearance of other days! When he arrived before his ancient home he looked—and saw nothing but a heap of bricks and stones! Such a sight threw him into a state of complete despondency.

He had no longer a roof nor a refuge. He was therefore obliged to seek lodging in an inn. After having left his things there he went to seek news of his family.

There were few inhabitants and these were thinly scattered; as they greeted him each recounted the events that had most impressed themselves upon his memory, and as each reached the point where his own heart had been wounded, torrents of tears bathed his face. "I wished," said Chin in his turn, "to come back and settle at home, but little did I think that my house was nothing but a heap of ruins! Alas! I have no home left!"

"Since the military revolts have broken out," replied his relations, "how many persons have been violently separated—the father to the south, the son to the north; some prisoners, others killed! As for us we have had to suffer misfortunes without end; and if all of us have escaped the point of the sword, that threatened us, it is but with difficulty we have managed to live. You rich people, grand gentlemen, whom no business obliged to remain, you have simply abandoned your houses, and nothing disagreeable has happened to you! Besides, the property you left we have taken care of. Thanks to us, you find your lands as you left them. If, then, you wish to settle again in this town, repair the damage that has been done, and you will still have enough to furnish a grand house." Chin

received this advice with thanks. He bought a house
in which to live, got all that was necessary to furnish
it, arranged a garden, and lived there quietly and
peaceably. Two months had passed in this way, when
Chin, having gone to the door of his house, saw a
man coming from the East and evidently coming to
his house, and in mourning from head to foot. In
spite of the bundle fastened to his shoulders, the man
walked as if he had wings, and presently was beside
him. Chin raised his eyes, and looked—what a surprise! It was Lew, a servant from his own house.

"Where do you come from, Lew? and what mean
these mourning-clothes?" said Chin Wang.

Directly he heard himself named, the servant made
haste to answer: "Ah, here you are, Sir. I was ordered to look for you till I died."

"But tell me, what is the meaning of your dress?"

"Here is a letter, Sir, a letter that will tell you
all." And the servant, putting his bundle on the
ground, took from it a letter. Chin hastened to break
the seals; he saw it was the writing of his mother,
and letter ran as follows:—

"After your departure we heard of the second revolt. Worn out
with anxiety night and day I soon fell seriously ill. Medicine and prayers are in vain; sooner or later we must all be written in the book
of the dead! But I am already over sixty, and there will be nothing
premature about my death. Only, I grieve over the troubles that
have broken out in this fatal year, and which force me to die a
stranger in a distant country, without you or your younger brother
being able to render me the last offices! I feel deeply unhappy about

this. I do not wish to be buried far away; yet I think with terror of the rebellion I fear that the Capital will not so soon recover its ancient state of tranquility, and that it is not now inhabitable: thus in my dying moments I have thought that you would do well to leave your ruined property, and to return here and occupy yourself with my funeral. After you have buried my body in the place designed for it, go to the East of the River: there is a fertile and populous country; the manners of the inhabitants are gentle and friendly: besides, how difficult would it be to re-establish yourself in the Capital on the same footing as before. Therefore wait till the sword and buckler may be laid aside, and then you may think again of going to the Capital. If you disobey my orders you will bring upon yourself a series of misfortunes in which you will be overwhelmed: you would make all your prayers and sacrifices by my grave useless, and even when you should come to the land of the Nine Fountains,* we should not be reunited.

"Read and mark this!"

On reading this Chin fell on the ground sobbing, "I hoped by coming here to re-establish my family in its ancient splendour, and to live in my own country, and, on the contrary, grief and anxiety caused by my absence bring my mother to her grave And if I had but known sooner! But I cannot arrive in time! All is over! My regrets are useless." After having lamented himself in this way, he asked the servant if his mother had not sent him any further counsels with her dying breath.

"No," answered Lew; "only she dwelt upon this, that all your property is in ruins here, and that things will grow worse through the last revolt, and that

* The other world.

therefore, Sir, you ought to leave this city, and go and occupy yourself with the care of the funeral. If my master were to refuse to obey the wishes of his dying mother, the poor lady would not be able to close her eyes in peace."

"How should I dare not to obey the directions of my dying mother?" cried Chin. "Besides, the country to the East of the River is very pleasant, whilst the Capital is a prey to incessant civil wars. It is much the best to fly this city."

And immediately he made haste to get his mourning-clothes ready, and to have the coffin made. On the one hand, he sent men to prepare the earth for the tomb, and, on the other, he gave orders to sell his house and land.

After having remained two days, the servant Lew objected that all these preparations of raising a tomb and surrounding it with an earthen wall would take a whole month, and as they were expecting him with impatience in the South, it would be better if he went on first to tranquilise their minds. Chin Wang approved of this, and had had the same idea. He wrote a letter, gave it to the servant with all the money he needed, and sent him off. Whilst he stood by the threshold, the servant said again to his master, "Although I go first, your Excellency will not forget to leave this place as quickly as possible and return to your own people."

"Alas!" replied Chin. "Would that I were free, and could fly home at once!" Then the servant went away.

Directly they learnt this news, Chin's relations came to condole with him, and to advise him not to lose too much upon his lands by selling them hastily. But, tormented by the last wishes of his mother, Chin persisted and would not listen to them: in his eagerness he sold his valuable lands for half their value. It was all he could do to wait twenty days to raise the hillock and hollow the tomb. As soon as everything was finished he arranged his baggage, and set off, followed by his servant. By starlight, through the middle of the night, he hurried quickly on, impatient to meet the procession, and to watch over the funeral rites. Alas!

> This journey to the Capital, made bravely, leaves him mourning.
> Now that with changed resolve towards the South he is returning!
> 'Twas vain that in the Capital he dreamed such brilliant dreams;
> 'Tis Heaven causes tears to flow, commands the sun's bright gleams.

II.

WE will now leave Chin to continue his journey, and will return to his mother and his wife, who had stayed behind at home. The news of the new Revolt had reached these two ladies, who passed their days and nights in anxiety and sadness, thinking of their son and husband, and repenting bitterly having let him set out. Two or three months had passed, when one day one of their servants came to say that Fo, the faithful servant of the absent master, had arrived from the Capital with a letter. On hearing this the ladies ordered Fo to enter, which he did, touching the ground with his forehead as he handed the letter. They noticed that poor Fo had completely lost his left eye; but without taking time to question him about this, the ladies opened the letter and read as follows:

"Since I left you, thanks to the protection of heaven I have always had excellent health. Happily, all our property has escaped in the Capital, and everything is in a satisfactory condition, as it used to be. To make it better, I met my old friend Hou-Pa, the judge, who introduced me to the Prime Minister, and I have every reason to be grateful to him, for he has appointed me to an important Magistracy. I have already received my official nomination, and as the time, at which I ought to enter on my duties is drawing near, I send Fo on purpose to give you both this letter. Directly you have received it make haste to sell our property, and come like lightning to the Capital. Do not waste time over frivolous details, it is all but time for me to start, and as we shall meet so soon this letter contains only what it is necessary to tell you. Chin salutes you a thousand times."

When the two ladies had read this letter, they could not contain their joy, and they then asked Fo how he had got his eye into such a sad condition. "It is scarcely worth speaking about," said the servant: "I was so tired out I fell asleep on horseback and happened to have a fall, in which I hurt myself." Then they asked him how the Capital looked, was it just as it used to be, were their relations all well? To these questions he answered: "The town is at least half in ruins, it is altogether changed. Some of your relations are dead, some are prisoners, others have taken flight, very few houses are standing whole; and of them, some have been robbed of their furniture and precious things, some are burnt and destroyed, others confiscated: your house and garden are the only ones that have suffered absolutely nothing."

These new details increased the joy and satisfaction of the two ladies.

"What!" cried they. "Our goods have not been touched, and Chin is appointed to a Magistracy! So much happiness is due to the protection of the supreme Ruler of heaven and earth: we cannot do enough to shew Him our gratitude. When the right moment comes we must shew it to Him by doing Good Works, and we must redouble our prayers on this occasion, so that in future the Magistracies may become more important, and our prosperity and appointments go on always increasing." Then they went on, addressing Fo: "This Judge, Hou-Pa, who is he?"

"He is a friend of my master's," said the servant.

"Till now," said Chin's mother, "I never heard of a Judge of this name, a friend of my son's."

"It is perhaps some new acquaintance of my husband's," said her daughter-in-law, "with whom we have never had anything to do."

Fo, taking part in the conversation, assured the ladies that the Judge in question was really a new acquaintance of his master's, and he asked them to give him an answer quickly. Chin's mother objected that after such a tiring journey he ought at least to rest till next day.

"Madam," said Fo, "the arrangements that you will have to make before starting will necessarily take some days. My master is alone, he has no one to wait upon him; he is impatient for someone to arrive to get everything in order for his departure; and if I wait till you, Madam, are ready, how can my master arrive in time to undertake his new appointment?"

Chin's mother thought this was reasonable; she wrote the answer wanted, gave the servant the money he needed for the journey, and sent him off. Directly

Fo had gone, the old lady set to work to sell all they owned in the Province, lands, houses, and furniture, and only kept a few trifles. In her fear of being too late she did not wait to get a good price for all things. The half of what she received she gave to a priest as a thank-offering, telling him to spend it in charity. Then she hired a Mandarin's boat, and carefully chose a lucky hour for setting out. During the last part of their stay their house was full from morning to night of young ladies from the neighbourhood, who came to take leave of them; all came to see the mother and wife of Chin Wang off in their boat.

Leaving their old home they travelled joyously along till they got into the Great River, when their boat went straight on towards the Capital. The servants of the two ladies, to celebrate the appointment of their Master to such an important charge, danced upon the deck! And yet it was not a moment for such rejoicing!

But now let us return to Chin, whom we left turning his back upon the Capital and hurrying on. It took him not quite a day to get to the place of embarcation. There he had his baggage put in the inn, sent away his beasts of burden, and, after having eaten, sent Fo, his servant, to hire a boat. He himself, seated at the door of the inn, was watching over his baggage, when in the middle of the stream he sees a boat advancing. He looked again ;—it is a Mandarin's

boat coming up against the current; at the prow
are four or five servants, who shew their joy by
shouts and songs, and who seem overflowing with
mirth and merriment. The boat keeps on advancing.
And Chin Wang looks again! These are not strangers!
why! these men are his own servants! He is as-
tounded "How is it that my servants are on a Mandarin's boat? Oh, on my mother's death they must
have passed into another service!" And whilst he is
still doubting and wondering a young girl comes before the carved screen, that closes the door of the
cabin, puts her head out, and looks. Chin looks at her
with an attentive and scrutinising gaze; it is his
wife's maid.

"Really! this is astonishing," thought Chin Wang.
With a quick step he springs forward to have an
explanation of this mystery, and at the same moment
all the people on the deck of the boat cry out together: "Why! our Master is here! How is this?
And what is the meaning of his mourning-clothes?"
They at once told the Captain to bring his boat along
shore, and in their surprise ran to the state cabin to
tell the two ladies, who raised the bamboo blind, and
looked out.

Then Chin suddenly saw his mother alive and
well. At once he tore off his sackcloth clothes, and
took from his Holdall other more fitting garments,
also a Cap; whilst all his servants, having sprung on

have been the cunning rogue who wrote these magical words?"

When Chin heard of a pretended Fo who had gone from him to his mother, his fear and surprise reached their height. "But my servant Fo has never left my side!" he exclaimed. "He has come here with me! When did he take a letter from me to my mother?"

The two ladies in their turn gave a cry of surprise. "Really, this is odder than ever," they said. "Last month your servant Fo brought us word that our property had remained uninjured in the midst of the ruins of the Capital, and that a certain Judge, whom you had met by chance, had introduced you to the Prime Minister, who had appointed you to a Magistracy; in short, that you desired us to sell everything, and to travel to the Capital quick as lightning, because you were on the point of setting out to undertake high office. After having got rid of our property we hired a boat and set out. And now you say your servant never made the journey to come to us!" Chin Wang was confounded. "This is some sorcerer's work," he said. "What Judge do I know? Who has ever introduced me to the Prime Minister? Have I ever been appointed to an office? Have I ever written you a letter?"

"But then," said his mother, "can there be a false Fo? Call him quickly. I want to question him."

"He is gone to hire a boat," said Chin, "but he will not be long in coming back."

All the servants gathered together at the prow, and soon they saw Fo coming running, dressed from head to foot in mourning; they call him, they make signs to him, and the poor fellow, who recognises them, asks himself in his astonishment what chance can have brought them here. He comes nearer, and as he does so the servants see at once that there is a difference between this Fo and that of a few days ago, and that is that the left eye of the pretended messenger was in a deplorable state, whilst the real Fo turns a pair of large bright eyes full of astonishment upon them. "Fo," they cry out from the edge of the boat, "the other day your left eye was in a bad way, how is it you have got it quite well now."

"You mean," cried Fo ironically, "that you yourselves have gone blind. Where did you see me the other day? Are you talking like this to bring a mischief upon me and make me lose the sight of an eye?"

"Decidedly," said the other servants smiling, "there is some witchcraft in this affair. The mother of your master wants to see you in her cabin. Take off quickly your mourning-clothes and go to see her."

At these words the servant stood stock still. "What! the mother of my master is yet alive! is here!"

"But," answered the servants, "where would she be, not to be here?"

have been the cunning rogue who wrote these magical words?"

When Chin heard of a pretended Fo who had gone from him to his mother, his fear and surprise reached their height. "But my servant Fo has never left my side!" he exclaimed. "He has come here with me! When did he take a letter from me to my mother?"

The two ladies in their turn gave a cry of surprise. "Really, this is odder than ever," they said. "Last month your servant Fo brought us word that our property had remained uninjured in the midst of the ruins of the Capital, and that a certain Judge, whom you had met by chance, had introduced you to the Prime Minister, who had appointed you to a Magistracy; in short, that you desired us to sell everything, and to travel to the Capital quick as lightning, because you were on the point of setting out to undertake high office. After having got rid of our property we hired a boat and set out. And now you say your servant never made the journey to come to us!" Chin Wang was confounded. "This is some sorcerer's work," he said. "What Judge do I know? Who has ever introduced me to the Prime Minister? Have I ever been appointed to an office? Have I ever written you a letter?"

"But then," said his mother, "can there be a false Fo? Call him quickly. I want to question him."

"He is gone to hire a boat," said Chin, "but he will not be long in coming back."

All the servants gathered together at the prow, and soon they saw Fo coming running, dressed from head to foot in mourning; they call him, they make signs to him, and the poor fellow, who recognises them, asks himself in his astonishment what chance can have brought them here. He comes nearer, and as he does so the servants see at once that there is a difference between this Fo and that of a few days ago, and that is that the left eye of the pretended messenger was in a deplorable state, whilst the real Fo turns a pair of large bright eyes full of astonishment upon them. "Fo," they cry out from the edge of the boat, "the other day your left eye was in a bad way, how is it you have got it quite well now."

"You mean," cried Fo ironically, "that you yourselves have gone blind. Where did you see me the other day? Are you talking like this to bring a mischief upon me and make me lose the sight of an eye?"

"Decidedly," said the other servants smiling, "there is some witchcraft in this affair. The mother of your master wants to see you in her cabin. Take off quickly your mourning-clothes and go to see her."

At these words the servant stood stock still. "What! the mother of my master is yet alive! is here!"

"But," answered the servants, "where would she be, not to be here?"

Fo would not believe a word of it, and refused to lay aside his mourning; he went hurriedly to the door of the cabin, but there his master stopped him with a severe voice: "Wretch! my mother is alive, she is here, and you do not lay aside these clothes to appear before her!" The poor servant then went out quickly to change his clothes, and came back in a more suitable dress to prostrate himself before the mother of his master.

Then the old lady rubbed and rubbed her old eyes. "A miracle!" she cried. "Fo, who came to us the other day, had a serious wound in his left eye, and now his sight is perfectly right! Certainly the man of the other day could not be he." Then she hastened to get out the letter, opened it—it was neither more nor less than blank paper without a trace of writing!

They were all troubled and surprised: they could not understand these transformations, nor the tricks that had been played upon them. But through this double trick, the Wang family was nearly ruined, and at the same time they feared fresh roguery of the same kind. Thus they were quite upset, and did not know what to count upon. Chin himself remained half the day buried in deep thought; then thinking of this pretended Fo with his left eye hurt, an idea came into his head, and, although not quite sure, he guessed rightly, and cried out; "That's it! I understand.

It must be that wretch of a Fox who has thus disguised himself to deceive me!"

"What do you mean?" asked his mother. Chin then told about his adventure in the forest, the arrival of the wounded Fox at the inn, how he had begged for his book during the night, and of his complaints in the courtyard of the inn, and he added: "I understood at the time that the enraged animal had changed itself into a man to get back its book, but not foreseeing how far its cunning would reach I was not in a position to defend myself."

At these words all the servants shook their heads and bit their tongues. "These Foxes," said they, "have wonderful powers of injuring people! In spite of the distance, they have been able to get up the same writing and the same appearance to deceive this separated family. If God had but pleased to make our master know what threatened him, then he would have given up the book, and all would have gone well!"

"No!" said Chin, "that I have had to suffer from the insolence of these wicked beasts is but another reason for keeping beside me this mysterious book; if new misfortunes come round me I shall throw into the fire this miserable source of so much sorrow!" "Alas!" interrupted his wife, "things have come to such a pass that we must not talk idly. Where are we to live now, I don't know. And besides, what means of living yet remain to us?"

"Our possessions in the Capital are sold," said Chin. "I don't know what to do! Besides, it is a long way to go there; it would be best to go to our home in the south."

"But," cried his mother in her turn "we have no home in the south, all is sold, where are we to live?" "Since circumstances oblige us, we must just hire a house, and establish ourselves in it," said Chin. Thereupon they turned the prow of the boat round, and went back again. The servants, who had set out with so much gaiety and enthusiasm, returned silent and cast down. Like a puppet whose strings are broken, their feet and their hands fell down without movement, and not a word came from their mouths; they who had come out in the exultation of triumph went back in the humiliation of defeat.

Chin disembarked first from the boat on their arrival. A little way from their previous home he hired a house, and after having spent some days furnishing got it ready for his mother and his wife. Then when he had done all, overpowered by anger, and crushed by grief, he would not go out, but sat at home brooding over his wrongs.

The neighbours, however, surprised to see again the ladies, of whom they had so lately taken leave, came in crowds to know the reason of their coming back, and Chin had to satisfy all their questions. Their adventures were reckoned marvellous, and every one talked about them.

One day as Chin was sitting in the large hall, watching his people at work, he saw a man come quickly up from outside; a man whose appearance was grave and majestic, his clothes elegant and well arranged. Now what he saw was:—

"A man wearing on his head a black silk cap such as was the fashion in those days, and a long green silk robe. Blue stones and bits of jade were sparkling round his cap, and long strips of silk of different shades were hanging from his girdle to the edge of his ample tunic. His white silk stockings were like two white clouds shining like snow, and the soles of his sandals were as brilliant as two clouds purpled by the sun. His appearance was imposing and had an elegance that was almost more of heaven than earth; the necklaces rising and falling on his chest would make hoarfrost grow red with envy. If not some great magician inhabiting the skies, he must be at least a monarch among men."

The stranger walked straight in and, as he looked at him, Chin recognised his younger brother Say. The latter greeted him affectionately, and asked how he had been since they last met.

"My wise brother," said Chin replying to his politenesses, "I am glad you have come here to look for me."

"When I arrived at the Capital," said Say, "I found our property changed into a desert, and I exclaimed: 'Now if he too has been crushed in the miseries of this civil war, what a misfortune it will be!' I asked our friends and relations, and I heard that you had gone South to seek a refuge: they told me that but a few days before you had been in the Capital, when the news of the desperate condition of our mother led you to start off at night by the light of the stars. On arriving here I went first to knock at your former house, but the neighbours told me you had moved here. However, our mother, I hear, is in good health, so I have been back to the boat to take off my mourning. But why, since she, whom we believed dead, is alive, have you come to live in this house, which does not appear yet habitable?"

"All that can not be told so quickly," said Chin: "but come and see my mother, and in talking with her you will learn all about us." Thereupon he took his brother to the old lady, whom the servants had already informed of the arrival of Say. Now when she knew that her younger son had come back, Say's mother was in the seventh Heaven of joy; she hastened forward to meet him, he threw himself at the feet of her from whom he had been so long absent, and when he rose, she said to him: "My son, day and night I have thought of you! But how have you been during this long absence?" Say thanked his mother, and then, while waiting to see his sister-in-law, begged to hear from her lips the details of all they had gone through.

Their conversation was interrupted by the arrival of Chin's wife, and then Chin began to tell all the story of the Foxes and what had come of it.

"Believe me," said Say, "all that was arranged from the beginning of the world; therefore, reproach only yourself, not those poor animals, that these misfortunes have come upon you. These two Foxes were quietly reading their book, and you—you were passing along the high road, so they did not disturb you in any way. Why then did you ill-use them? Why steal their book from them? Afterwards in the inn they came to tell you their grief, how unhappy they were over their loss; they came to get their book back, but you were determined they should not have it. Then why again this wicked thought of seizing your sword to kill them? And when they came with stern but faithful words to beseech you, once again you refused obstinately. Yet, if you will but consider, you can't read a word of this book, never in all your life will it be of any use to you, why then keep it? Now you see your affairs are in a deplorable state, and you have no one to blame but yourself."

"That is just what I tell my husband," said Chin's wife. "Of what use can this book ever be to us? And see what a sea of troubles it has plunged us into!"

To these reproaches of his younger brother Chin answered not a word, but he felt hurt in his heart. "And this book," asked Say, "is it large? In what characters is it written?"

"It is big enough," replied the elder brother, "but

as to what there is in it, I know nothing about it, for there is not even a letter that I know."

"Let me look at it," said Say. "Yes," said his sister-in-law, "go and get it for your brother to examine, perhaps he will be more skilful to read it, who knows."

"I can well believe," said Say, "that it is a very difficult writing to read, but I should like to see these pages just as a curiosity, that is all."

Chin went to fetch the book, and put it into the hands of his brother; the latter took it, turned it round and round, and examined it from top to bottom. "Yes," said he, "it is true these are letters such as one seldom sees." Then he rose, crossed the room, and walked straight up to Chin saying: "The Lew of the other day was I myself. Now that I again hold in my hands this sacred book, I will not torment you any more—Farewell—Be at peace." With these words he went out, running swift as light.

In the fury of his anger Chin rushed after the supernatural being, crying with all his might: "Audacious animal, where are you going?" And with one hand he seized him by his clothes; the fugitive struggled violently, but Chin held him with a powerful hand. Then they heard him murmur some strange words. Chin tore the clothes off the fairy animal, which shook itself violently, and then appeared as a Fox, running away as hard as it could, and disappearing like a whirlwind. Chin with all his servants ran down the street after him, but could find no trace of him.

First ruined, then insulted by the Fox, Chin was enraged at the loss of the book in their third meeting. Gnashing his teeth, he looked from side to side to try to see his enemy. He saw nothing! Nothing but an old priest, blind of one eye, sitting at his door under the shadow of the projecting eaves, and when he asked him in which direction the Fox had gone, the old man only raised his arm and pointed to the East. Chin and his people rushed headlong in that direction, but they had barely run the length of five or six houses, when the old man cried out: "Chin Wang, the Fo of the other day was I myself! Your younger brother is here."

On hearing these words the whole troop rushed back. The two Foxes, holding the book they had got back, went dancing along before their enemies to annoy them. Chin's servants ran as hard as they could; but the two Foxes put their four feet to the ground, and fled as if they had wings.

Chin had got back as far as his own door chasing after them, when his mother cried out, "The book, which has caused all our misery and ruined us, is gone! Let them alone! Let them be! If you run after them, they are far away already, and will never give it back to you." Then Chin, in spite of the anger which choked him, was obliged to listen to his mother, and he came back with all his servants following him. His first care was to examine the clothe left by the Fox, but hardly had he touched them before they were all changed. If you wish to know what remained, here it is:—

"A banana-leaf, which had looked like a silk gown! Old water-lily stalks had made the silk cap. The bits of jade, the shining blue stones, were nothing but little bits of wood cut out of a decaying willow. That plant of which rain mantles are woven together, represented the long silk strips hanging from the girdle; the silken socks were white paper, and the beautiful soles of the sandals two bits of old fir-tree bark."

This sight threw them all into fresh astonishment. They exclaimed, "Oh wonder of wonders! These Foxes are indeed fairies, since they have such a wonderful power. And who knows where our young master really is, since it was only an apparition, this, that looked like him." Thus spoke the servants, while Chin, what with grief and anger, got a violent attack of fever, and went to bed. His mother sent for the doctor, and we will leave him in their hands.

Some days had passed, when the servants, who were in the large hall, which looked on to the street, saw a traveller arriving, who was, as they thought at the first glance, Say, the brother of their master. His black silk cap, his woven tunic were exactly like the dress of the Fairy Fox. "Without doubt," said they, "this must be the false Say Wang." And they all began to cry at once: "Here is the Fairy Fox!

here he is!" Then each seizing a stick with both hands, they set upon the new-comer, and began to belabour him with blows. "You scoundrels!" cried Say in a rage, "why do you receive me in this way instead of going to announce me to my mother, as you ought to do?" But the servants continued their amiable greeting, on which Say, being naturally violent, snatched a cudgel from one of them, and, rushing in among them, knocked down five or six. The others did not dare approach him after this, but, drawing back, stood at the door inside the room pointing at him, and insulting him: "You wicked animal!" they shouted. "Since you have got your book back, what are you come to do here?"

It was impossible for Say to understand what they meant, so he pushed rudely on towards his mother's room, whilst the servants, retreating before him, by their cries and noise. frightened the old lady, who surprised to hear such a tumult at her door, came hurrying out. "It is the Fairy Fox," shouted the terrified servants. "Look at him, just like our young master. He comes in — he comes on in spite of us." "How now! can it be true?" said, in her turn, Say's mother. And she had not finished speaking, when her son stood before her eyes. On seeing the old lady, he threw down at once the cudgel, with which he was armed, and bowed to the ground before her. "Mother," said he, "why do these ruffians of servants attack me

with sticks, pretending that I am a Fairy Fox?"
"Are you really my son?" she asked. "Why yes, I
am the child you brought into the world," said the
young man. "Is there then a pretended Say Wang?"

In the midst of this conversation seven or eight
strange servants brought Chin's brother's baggage; and
convinced then that their young master was really
before them, the servants came to knock their fore-
heads on the ground at his feet, and to excuse themselves. "But what does it all mean then?" asked Say
again. Then his mother told him the story of the
enchanted Foxes, and that his brother was seriously
ill, and not getting at all better so far.

"Well, but then," interrupted Say, surprised and
frightened, "I have as much to tell you. Whilst I was
away, ever so far off in the land of Cho, your servant
came to bring me a letter. Without doubt he was
nothing but one of these Foxes."

"And what did this letter say?" "You know," said
Say, "that I went to the land of Cho in the suite of
the Emperor, simply as one of his guards. There I
obtained a second command, and that was why your
younger son could not accompany the Emperor when
he returned to the Capital, but remained beyond the
frontier. Two months ago a pretended Lew brought
me a letter from my elder brother, announcing to me
that he had gone south, that our mother was dead,
and begging me to come for the funeral. This pre-

tended Lew wanted to start at once for the Capital himself to prepare the grave, and set off before me at day-break, whilst I took leave of my chief and set out, leaving there many little things of value and only taking with me what was strictly necessary. When I reached your former house I learnt from the neighbours that my mother was alive, and I hastened to the boat to lay aside my mourning. And now here I am! But I should like to hear from my brother himself who it is who has taken delight in alarming us and deceiving us with false news, for, in truth, I don't understand these incredible adventures in the least."

Thereupon he opened his packages, and got out the letter, but it was nothing but a piece of blank paper, which made them all, however, more inclined to laugh than to fret about it.

Say went in with his mother to his sister-in-law's room, and asked to see Chin. But poor Chin was delirious: "My son," then said his old mother, "these mischievous Foxes have done us much harm, but I forgive them for having played you this trick and brought you back from the land of Cho. At least they are the cause that mother and son are reunited, and by this good deed alone their faults are atoned for! We must not be too hard upon the Foxes."

For two months Chin was in raging fever, then he began to get better. They called him in all the country

round the "Robber," because he had robbed the Foxes
of their book that they loved above their life.

The Serpent creeps, the Tiger springs; each brute has his device;
The Foxes sacred books possess, and hold beyond all price.
Whilst houses fall and goods are lost, and the books too
    disappear;
Yet will men laugh at poor Chin Wang for many a thousand
    year!

LIST OF BOOKS

ON CRÊPE PAPER WITH ILLUSTRATIONS IN COLOURS.

T. HASEGAWA,

Publisher, Printer & Crêpe Paper Manufacturer,
10 HIYOSHICHO, TOKIO, JAPAN.

T. HASEGAWA undertakes the printing and binding of all kinds of Japanese Artistic Books, Pamphlets etc. on CRÊPE and other fine paper. CIRCULARS, CATALOGUES, PRICE LISTS etc. printed on CRÊPE PAPER manufactured on the Establishment, and Japanese Art Designs furnished. Estimates and orders will receive prompt attention.

明治廿七年十一月一日印刷
明治廿七年十一月十日發行

發行者兼
繪蒔印刷者

東京京橋區日吉前十番地

長谷川武次郎

著者　英國人

リットル夫人

東京日本橋區卯町二番地東京製紙分社

印刷者　齋藤常達

版權所有